My Best is Good Enough

By Ramont and Zion Mittchell

Illustrated by Arsal. K

This book belongs to

_____

My name is Zion.

I love baseball.

I love to hit the ball hard
and run around
the bases and slide in
to home plate to
make the winning run.

But sometimes if I miss the ball, I get upset.

My dad says to me, "Zion, the only way to get better is to keep swinging.

Your best will always be good enough."

I love to play tennis.
Tennis is so much fun.

I like running back and forth
to hit the ball over the net.

When I hit the ball
into the net or out of bounds
it makes me frustrated.

When that happens my dad
says, "Zion, trust your work.
Your best will always be
good enough."

I am super fast in track.
I can run really, really fast.

As soon as someone says,
"go", I know that I can get
to the finish line first.

If I don't get to the finish
line first, I feel like
I didn't do well.

My dad never lets me quit.
He always says,
"Zion just run your best race.

Your best will
always be good enough."

I love to play soccer.
I can score lots of goals.

I can play goalie
and block kicks.

If I let a goal past me into the net, it makes me sad. I never want to let my team down.

My dad always tells me "Zion, you can't play well when you are sad. Do the best that you can do.

Your best will always be good enough."

I love basketball too.
I can dribble.
I can shoot.
I can score the ball
in the hoop.

But sometimes I miss too many shots and I feel like they will never go in.

My dad says, "Zion, you will miss all of the shots you don't take.

Do your best and it will always be good enough."

After every game,
my dad asks me two things.

He asks, "did you have fun?"

And he asks,
"did you try your best?"

He tells me, "Winning is great,
but it won't always happen.

As long as you gave it your all,
your best will
always be good enough."

I know that my dad loves me no matter what happens in the game.

My best is good enough.

Made in the USA
Coppell, TX
31 December 2020